Lex Luthor
AND THE
KRYPTONITE CAVERNS

SUPER
DC
HEROES
VILLAINS

WRITTEN BY
J.E. BRIGHT

ILLUSTRATED BY
LUCIANO VECCHIO

SUPERMAN CREATED BY
JERRY SIEGEL AND
JOE SHUSTER

Raintree is an imprint of Capstone Global Library Limited, a company incorporated in England and Wales having its registered office at 7 Pilgrim Street, London, EC4V 6LB - Registered company number: 6695582

To contact Raintree please phone 0845 6044371, fax + 44 (0) 1865 312263, or email myorders@raintreepublishers.co.uk. Customers from outside the UK please telephone +44 1865 312262.

First published by Stone Arch Books in 2012
First published in the United Kingdom in 2013
The moral rights of the proprietor have been asserted.

Originated by Capstone Global Library Ltd
Printed and bound in China by Leo Paper Products Ltd

ISBN 978 1 406 26667 2
18 17 16 15
10 9 8 7 6 5 4 3

British Library Cataloguing in Publication Data
A full catalogue record for this book is available from the British Library.

CONTENTS

CHAPTER 1
UNDERGROUND AMBUSH 6

CHAPTER 2
CREEPY CRAWLERS 16

CHAPTER 3
DISMANTLING SUPERMAN 24

CHAPTER 4
THE FLAW IN THE PLAN 33

CHAPTER 5
REVERSAL 43

BIOGRAPHIES 52

GLOSSARY 53

DISCUSSION QUESTIONS 54

WRITING PROMPTS 55

LEX LUTHOR

REAL NAME: Lex Luthor

OCCUPATION: Mastermind

HEIGHT: 1.88 metres

WEIGHT: 95 kilograms

EYES: Green

HAIR: None

BIOGRAPHY:

Lex Luthor is one of the richest and most powerful people in all of Metropolis. He's known as a successful businessman to most, but Superman knows Luthor's dirty little secret – most of his wealth is ill-gotten, and behind the scenes he is a criminal mastermind. Superman has stopped many of Luthor's sinister schemes, but Lex is careful to avoid getting caught red-handed. Lex wants to control Superman to strengthen his grip on Metropolis, but the Man of Steel is immune to Luthor's influence.

Superior intelligence

Battle suit

Energy blaster

Jet boots

POWERS/ABILITIES:
Skilled fighter; quickly
masters new equipment;
fuelled by extreme rage.

CHAPTER 1

UNDERGROUND AMBUSH

Lex Luthor, after all his years of trying, had finally discovered a foolproof method to destroy Superman.

"Chrome, report," Lex said. He gazed at his newest secret weapon, which was housed in a large lead dome.

An elegant silver hover-bot, floating above the dome, flew down and bobbed in the air beside Lex. Chrome was shaped like a long bowling pin, with a single camera eye on top, and a retractable multi-purpose claw extending from its middle.

"Reporting," Chrome answered in a female-sounding electronic voice. "Preparation is ninety-nine percent complete. All five cave areas functional and ready. Ultimate weapon powered and ready. Lure signal online and ready. Control Centre operational, but needs the presence of Lex Luthor to be complete."

"Perfect," Lex replied. A shiver of excitement ran through his muscles. It was almost time to destroy the alien menace who had controlled Earth for decades – the menace known as Superman.

Lex and Chrome were in a large cavern system miles below the surface of a desert in Utah. Five smaller caves connected along a twisting path that led down to this, the largest cave. The cavern was thirty metres wide.

The cave had a high ceiling that was studded with pointy, dripping stalactites, and a rocky floor covered with jagged stalagmites.

Lex took a deep breath and looked around at his preparations. It had taken more than a year's work and a big chunk of his wealth to build this trap. The cavern was perfect for his needs: it didn't appear on any map, the rock formations were naturally streaked with lead, and a thin trickling stream crossed the rock floor.

The ultimate weapon – a kryptonite plasma cannon – was housed in the lead dome, with only its muzzle showing. The stream trickled under the dome to cool the radioactive cannon. The weapon was powerful enough to destroy his enemy. . . if Superman was sufficiently weakened first.

"Chrome," Lex ordered, "give me a radiation report."

Chrome checked its internal Geiger counter. "Kryptonite radiation leakage minimal," the hover-bot reported. "Considered safe for human exposure. The water in the stream has become radioactive from the coolant runoff, but it does not present a hazard to Lex Luthor unless he should drink it."

"Excellent," Lex said.

Lex admired the lead dome that he had placed around the weapon. He had done so for two reasons.

The first was to shield himself from the kryptonite radiation leaking from the weapon. Kryptonite had done terrible things to Lex's body from many years of exposure to it.

Lex wasn't going to risk direct exposure to kryptonite ever again.

The second reason for the lead dome was to prevent Superman from seeing the weapon with his X-ray vision before Lex could fire it at him. The natural lead in the cavern walls helped hide the trap, too.

"We are ready to proceed," Chrome said, "if Lex Luthor will enter the Control Centre."

Lex nodded. "Let's begin," he said. He stepped over to a squat windowless building by the side of the dome, on the bank of the trickling stream. This was the Control Centre, which was also lined with lead. Lex opened the heavy door and stepped inside the cool room. It was filled with glowing computer monitors. "Initiate lockdown," he ordered Chrome through his wireless headset.

"Lockdown initiated," Chrome replied in his earpiece.

CLICK! CLICK! Lex heard the thick bolts sliding into place within the doorframe. The door – and the whole Control Centre structure – wouldn't keep out Superman under normal circumstances. But Lex had good reason to believe Superman would be greatly weakened by the time he reached it.

"Lex Luthor is secured within the Control Centre," Chrome reported. "Preparation is now one hundred percent complete. Ready and awaiting further instructions."

Lex peered down at the bank of computer monitors. They displayed video feeds from multiple hidden cameras above the ground, within the five smaller caves, and inside the larger cavern. He could switch to any angle in each area with the touch of a button.

Lex could see the weapon dome and the Control Centre, with Chrome hovering right outside.

The five smaller caves appeared calm and quiet, illuminated with soft lighting. But Lex had set up nasty surprises in each one that were designed to weaken the alien menace step by step.

The entire cave system was a Superman death trap.

"Final systems check," Lex said to Chrome.

"All systems online and ready," the hover-bot confirmed. "Lex Luthor can proceed at will."

With an excited flex of his fingers, Lex smiled. "Initiate lure," he commanded.

"Lure initiated," Chrome announced.

Lex couldn't hear it, but he knew that Chrome had triggered a loud, high-frequency signal near the cave's entrance. It was a recording of the bottled Kryptonian capital city of Kandor, which he had captured in the past and tried to destroy. Superman had rescued the alien city and hidden it away again, but not before Lex had recorded this very useful citywide cry of terror. It would act as a distress signal, a beacon that only Superman could hear – and couldn't possibly ignore.

The enemy alien would be arriving at any moment.

And then Lex would destroy him.

CHAPTER 2

CREEPY CRAWLERS

Lex stared intently at a radar screen that scanned the sky above the desert, watching for the first sign of Superman's arrival. So far, the airspace was clear, but the alien could appear at supersonic speed at any moment.

"Alert!" Chrome announced. "Reporting unplanned activity."

"What?" Lex barked. "Is Superman inside already?"

"Negative," replied Chrome.

"Cave creatures near the stream are engaged in unusually aggressive behaviour," Chrome explained. "There is also a spike in radioactivity."

CLINK CLINK From inside the Control Centre, Lex tapped the touchscreen to shift the camera view of the large cave over to the stream near the dome. He scanned the space, and zoomed in on a few moving spots that were glowing toxic green.

Sure enough, as Lex focused in closer, he could see a few creatures scurrying about by the edge of the stream. Lex zoomed in closer.

The little cave dwellers who lived in constant darkness were already strange – but these creatures were weirder than usual. A line of six albino cave spiders faced off against a pack of pale millipedes.

Ghostly blind salamanders hissed at a battalion of crickets and beetles. Cave crayfish had crawled up on the banks of the creek, clicking their claws. Around the edges, transparent scorpions marched forward, their stingers ready to strike.

Lex raised his eyebrows. The creatures were acting unusual. He wasn't sure he'd ever seen insects, arachnids, and amphibians so organized to fight. Each animal was glowing and most seemed larger than normal. They must have been affected by the kryptonite in the stream.

"Monitor the creatures," Lex instructed Chrome. "Alert me if anything changes."

Then Lex turned his focus back to the monitors showing the cave entrance. The critters were only a minor irritation, certainly nothing to worry about.

I have to save all my attention for Superman, Lex thought.

BEEP! BEEP! Alarms sounded from the computers. "ALIEN ARRIVAL," a pop-up message declared.

Lex opened his eyes wide as he scanned the monitors, which were shifting to find Superman's location. Two cameras locked in on the alien from opposite angles.

There he was – Superman, landing amidst the scrubby brush outside the cavern. He stood in the rocky landscape, the desert wind billowing his cape out behind him. Superman listened to Lex's distress call from Kandor, narrowed his eyes, and then flew into the air.

Superman soared directly into the mouth of the cavern, and the cameras swivelled to follow his progress.

CLICK! Lex switched over to a view of the first cave. Superman soared inside, dodging around stalactites and curtains of rock. When he reached the centre of the cave, he automatically set off the first trap.

ZZRRRRTT! A beam of green energy struck Superman from a laser hidden in the ceiling's rock formations. It was a gravity ray combined with a kryptonite filter that Lex had developed himself.

In mid-air, Superman writhed in pain. Then the ray took effect, increasing Superman's gravity a hundredfold. The alien dropped out of the air, slamming onto the cave floor with a **THUD!**

Lex grinned. He'd temporarily managed to remove Superman's power of flight! Superman struggled to crawl along the cave floor.

Superman still had his super-strength, so he picked himself off the ground and brushed himself off. He grimaced from the extra weight of his body due to the gravity ray. But he ventured on, going deeper into the cave towards the Kandor distress signal.

Lex smiled. "I knew he wouldn't give up," he said. "He never gives up, no matter what I throw at him."

Superman would persevere until the bitter end. . . where Lex would destroy him for good!

"Alert!" Chrome reported. "Radioactive creatures increasing in size."

Lex didn't even check on the strange animals on his monitor. He was too pleased that his plan was working so well.

CHAPTER 3

DISMANTLING SUPERMAN

Lex watched the monitor as Superman ducked under a crystal formation and entered the second cave in the cavern chain.

When the ceiling was high enough, Superman stood up straight. His eyes glowed red as he scanned the cramped rocky chamber with his X-ray vision. He must have spotted a piece of the camera, because he looked directly into it. "I don't know who you are," Superman said, "but I demand you return Kandor to me immediately! The people in that bottle are innocent!"

Lex sniggered. *Kandorians have no business being on Earth,* Lex thought, *even shrunk down in a bottle. Besides, they're actually safe, hidden away somewhere in your icy Fortress of Solitude.*

For a moment, Superman stared into the camera in the cave, waiting for some kind of response. When all he got was silence, he said, "After I rescue them myself, I'll bring you to justice." Then he zapped the camera with his heat vision. The monitor went blank.

Lex sighed. He switched the monitor to show the view from another camera hidden in the cave. There were many back-up cameras – he had planned this ambush well!

Lex touched an icon on the monitor screen and a mirrored disc descended from the roof of the cave above Superman.

As Lex expected, Superman glanced up and blasted it with his heat vision. The red laser beam shooting from the alien's eyes hit the mirrored disk. The disc flared with green energy, amplified the beam, and mixed it with kryptonite radiation. It shot a ray right back into Superman's eyes!

Superman pressed his hands to his face. *Bull's-eye!* Luthor thought, laughing.

When Superman lowered his hands, his eyes were tinged with green. Lex watched as the Man of Steel tried to use his X-ray vision, and. . . nothing happened. Lex had succeeded in shutting off another of Superman's alien powers!

Lex felt like letting out a whoop of triumph, but he reminded himself to stay calm and watch the monitors. There were more traps to spring.

"Alert!" Chrome squawked. "The mutated creatures continue to grow –"

"Not now, Chrome," Lex snapped. "I'm only concerned with reports that directly affect the operation."

"Yes, Lex Luthor," Chrome replied.

Lex stared intently at the monitor. Superman gritted his teeth and marched resolutely forward towards Cave Three. Lex held his breath while Superman made his way to the centre of the next cave.

Superman's movement triggered the next trap, which released four jets of hot vapour laced with kryptonite gas. The plumes of toxic steam hit Superman from all directions, and he couldn't help but inhale some of it.

Superman doubled over, coughing. Lex knew that the vapour had seared Superman's lungs.

It had limited his ability to use his freeze breath. Another power down! Even so, Superman kept striding into the caves. Lex admired the alien's determination.

At the entrance to the fourth cave, Superman paused. By this time, he knew that there would be another trap. But without his X-ray vision, he had no chance to see what was hidden all around him. Lex was particularly proud of this cave's machinery. Only a genius biochemist and an engineer like himself could have developed it. To hurry Superman along, Lex pressed a button, amplifying the volume of the recorded cries from Kandor.

Superman clenched his hands into fists and stepped inside Cave Four.

WHIR-WHIR-WHIR-WHIR!!

Vibrating sonic waves shot out of hidden speakers all around the cave. The noise resonated through kryptonite crystals, tuning the blare to the frequency of the radioactive mineral. These rays of sound throbbed through Superman's skin and attacked the energy-making molecules of his cells. This sound would weaken him significantly.

Superman slumped forward. Now he was as weak as an ordinary human. Lex lowered a steel door between Caves Four and Three. Without his super-strength, Superman couldn't escape. There would be no retreat for the alien.

"Why are you doing this?" Superman said, glaring around the cave. "Who are you?"

Lex shook his head and grinned.

Who else but Lex Luthor could create such an ingenious trap? Lex thought.

"I don't know who you are," Superman continued, "but I will do anything to rescue the people of Kandor. I will never give up!"

Of course not, Lex thought. The alien was so arrogant, so sure of his endurance, that he would always keep coming, no matter how weak he was. That arrogance was what Lex hated most about his old enemy.

Superman narrowed his eyes and headed towards Cave Five. Lex only had to remove one more major ability and Superman would be powerless as long as he remained in these caves.

CHAPTER 4

THE FLAW IN THE PLAN

Superman slid down a rocky ramp, then dropped into a hole that led to Cave Five. It made Lex smile to see Superman moving carefully, struggling to make his way through the tunnels.

When Superman entered the barren chamber of the fifth cave, he didn't pause like he had previously. He just kept walking. *Maybe he thinks he has nothing left to lose,* Lex thought. *But he does.*

Lex pressed an icon on his touchscreen, unleashing the fifth trap.

A fake-rock panel in the cave slid down, revealing an array of small bulbs arranged on a curved plate. These were no ordinary light bulbs – inside each one, a tiny nuclear fusion reaction was taking place, similar to the process that powered every star in the cosmos.

But Lex hadn't replicated the power of Earth's yellow sun. Instead, in each little bulb, he had created a small red star.

The array of red lights powered up and radiated a wide beam right at Superman. But Superman had heard the almost-silent movement of the panel. He jumped out of the way, rolling behind a fat stalagmite jutting up from the cave floor. He hid from the red light in the stalagmite's shadow.

Lex smacked his fist down on the monitor.

Lex hadn't bothered with removing Superman's super-hearing, figuring it wouldn't be much use. But it had alerted the alien to the solar radiation attack.

The power in the bulbs would only last a few minutes. Lex hadn't expected to need it for very long. He had to lure Superman out from behind the stalagmite somehow, or his entire plan would fail.

Lex calmed himself. There was one more trick he'd kept in reserve. With quick movements of his fingertips on the touchscreen, he started another recording from Kandor of a little boy crying to his mother. "Mummy," the boy whimpered, "why doesn't Kal-El save us? Has he forgotten about us? I'm so scared!"

Lex grinned as he saw Superman shudder behind the stalagmite.

There was no way Superman could resist what he thought was one of his own fellow aliens crying for help.

Sure enough, Superman shakily pulled himself to his feet. "You monster!" he bellowed as he stepped into the red solar light.

Superman grimaced as the light bathed his body. It wasn't strong enough to destroy him, but the radiation was sufficient to give Superman a wicked sunburn.

Weakened by red solar light, Superman lost the invulnerability that the yellow sun of Earth gave him. Trapped in these caves, the Man of Steel was now no more than an ordinary man.

Groaning, Superman lurched out of Cave Five. He staggered into the largest cave, and faced the Control Centre bunker.

"Come out of there and show yourself!" Superman cried. "I've taken all the punishment you can dish out! Now give me back the bottle of Kandor!"

Lex's hands trembled in excitement. *Not all the punishment,* he thought.

As Superman limped closer to the bunker, Lex fired the plasma cannon. *ZZAPPPPPPP!* The full force of the weapon hit Superman directly on the S in the centre of his uniform.

Superman screamed as the kryptonite plasma cannon began separating his molecules. In Superman's weakened state, it would destroy him in only a few minutes. Lex kept his eyes glued to the image on his monitor of the writhing Superman. He didn't want to miss a second of the destruction of his arch-enemy.

"Alert!" Chrome reported. "Mutated creatures burrowing into the bunker!"

"What?" Lex cried. He flicked a monitor to show the bunker. An army of green-glowing creatures was tunnelling under the lead dome. All kinds of creepy-crawlies were all digging together. And they weren't small anymore – they'd grown as large as rats.

"How did they get so big?" Lex cried. "Why didn't you warn me?"

"Lex Luthor gave orders," said Chrome, "not to bother him unless the creatures directly affected operation of –"

"Shut up, Chrome!" Lex yelled. "Stop them!"

Chrome floated over to the digging creatures. The hover-bot grabbed a giant scorpion with its claw.

The rest of the creatures swarmed all over Chrome and dragged it down to the cave floor.

"Alert!" Chrome squawked. "Under attack! Alert –"

It took only seconds for the mutated creatures to dismantle the hover-bot into metallic chunks. Then they quickly disappeared under the dome's wall and returned to their digging.

Lex gasped. Chrome had been an extremely expensive hover-bot to create.

Then Lex watched in horror as the plasma cannon's beam flickered, and sputtered out. The creatures must have ripped apart the electronics inside the dome. "No!" he yelled. "My weapon! My perfect weapon!"

Superman fell onto his back, sucking in deep breaths as he recovered from the plasma beam's attack.

He's almost as weak as a human now, Lex thought. *I'll just go face him myself!* Lex grabbed a utility wrench to use as a weapon.

With the touch of a button, the door of the Control Centre unbolted and slid open. Lex stepped out into the cave.

Suddenly, a swarm of oversized creatures surrounded Lex from behind the Control Centre. The spiders, scorpions, and beetles advanced slowly towards him, their eyes glowing with green fury.

CHAPTER 5

REVERSAL

Lex backed up against the dome wall. He swung the wrench wildly at the creatures, but he knew it wouldn't keep them away for long.

Lex was in terrible danger. He had seen what the creatures did to Chrome. As much as he hated the idea, there was only one thing that could save him. One person.

"Superman," Lex called. "Get me out of here!"

Superman sat up. "Lex Luthor," he groaned. "I should have known it was you behind all of this. Return Kandor to me!"

CRUNCH! Lex smacked a scorpion with his wrench. "I don't have the bottle," he admitted. "It was only a recording."

Superman blinked hard. "You did all this just to get to me?" he asked.

"I'd do anything to save Earth from an alien like you!" Lex yelled.

Superman crossed his arms. "That's just because you want to control Earth yourself," he said sternly. "I may be from another planet, but I love Earth. It's my home. The only one I have. And I'll always protect it from men like you."

The creatures had cornered Lex, trapping him against a wall of rock.

"Good for you!" Lex said. "We can only get back to the surface by working together. Distract these monsters!"

Superman nodded. He began throwing rocks at the creatures. They crawled away from Lex and headed towards Superman.

"Now run!" Lex shouted. He bolted towards the cave's exit, with Superman following close behind.

"How do we get through the steel door?" Superman asked as they ran.

"Leave that to me," Lex said, as they scrambled up the ramp to Cave Four. The creatures chased after them, their legs clicking eerily on the rocky floor.

In the fourth cave, Lex hurried over to a hidden control panel. "Hold the creatures off!" he ordered Superman.

While Superman hurled more rocks at the swarm, Lex quickly adjusted the settings on the panel. Then he started up the sonic weapon, but at a different frequency. The sound echoed out again, but this time it would return Superman's cells to normal energy production, reversing the earlier effect.

Superman's body shivered. "You have your super-strength back," Lex said. "Now rip that door open!"

Superman ran to the door and tore the thick steel into shreds. He and Lex raced through the opening, with the creatures hot on their heels. They sprinted through the next two chambers until they reached Cave One. Lex stopped in front of the gravity ray and opened the device's panel.

"Some of your superpowers won't come back until you are exposed to the yellow rays of the sun again," Lex explained as he manipulated the ray's circuitry. "However, I can give you back your flight right now by reversing the gravity ray's control."

Lex slammed the device's panel shut. Immediately, the ray of light illuminated a nearby wall. "I'll hold off the creatures while the ray takes effect," Lex said.

Superman nodded. He walked into the path of the beam and bathed in the laser's light. Soon, Superman could fly again. He grabbed Lex and carried him up and out of the cavern.

As they soared from the cave, Superman kicked the roof of the entrance, breaking off a huge chunk of rock. CRASH!!

It smashed into the cave's mouth, trapping the mutated creatures inside.

The Man of Steel soared higher into the air with Lex in his arms. "You do realize I'm taking you back to prison now, right?" Superman asked.

"Not a surprise," Lex replied.

But Lex had one last trick up his sleeve. Lex had grabbed a mutant scorpion and hidden it in his armour. He pulled out the squirming creature.

Superman hadn't been in the sun long enough to recharge all his powers. He was still vulnerable. The scorpion's radioactive venom might hurt him.

Lex grabbed onto the big, glowing scorpion and held it up to Superman. But the scorpion twisted, flailed his tail, and stung Lex on his hand.

"Ah!" Lex cried, quickly dropping the nasty creature.

Superman chuckled. "Not your best evil plan," he said.

Lex scowled. He opened his mouth to speak, but just then the toxic venom hit his bloodstream, making him feel truly awful.

"Take me. . . to the hospital," Lex said.

Superman flew faster over the desert. "First stop – Metropolis Hospital," he agreed. "But then you're going to jail for a long, long time."

Lex sighed. It was humiliating to be saved by someone he hated so much.

Mental note, Lex thought, as Superman carried him through the sky towards civilization. *Never ignore the little things. They'll ruin your biggest plans.*

BIOGRAPHIES

J.E. Bright is the author of many novels, novelizations, non-fiction books, and novelty books for children and young adults. He lives in a sunny apartment in New York, USA with his cats Mabel and Bernard.

Luciano Vecchio was born in 1982 and currently lives in Buenos Aires, Argentina. With experience in illustration, animation, and comics, his works have been published in the United Kingdom, United States, Spain, France, and Argentina. Credits include Ben 10 (DC Comics), Cruel Thing (Norma), Unseen Tribe (Zuda Comics), and Sentinels (Drumfish Productions).

GLOSSARY

ambush hide and then attack someone

dismantling taking something apart piece by piece

foolproof very simple and cannot easily go wrong

frequency number of cycles per second of a radio wave

functional working well or designed to work well

grimace make a facial expression indicating pain or displeasure

menace threat or danger

mutate change or alter

radioactive radioactive materials are made up of atoms whose nuclei break down, giving off harmful radiation

toxic poisonous, as in toxic waste

vulnerable weakened and likely to be hurt or damaged

DISCUSSION QUESTIONS

1. Why do you think Lex Luthor wants to stop Superman from protecting the world?

2. Superman risked his life to save the citizens of Kandor. Talk about times when you've done something for someone else.

3. This book has 10 illustrations. Which one was your favourite? Why?

WRITING PROMPTS

1. Lex built his secret base deep underground beneath the desert. If you could have a secret base, where would you put it? What would be inside it? Write about your secret base.

2. This book was told from Lex Luthor's perspective. Rewrite your favourite chapter of this story from Superman's point of view. What is he feeling? What is he thinking? Write about it.

3. Lex Luthor created his very own mechanical assistant. Imagine your own robotic friend. What does it look like? What does it help you do? Write about it, then draw a picture of it.